THE MEGAMOGS in Moggymania

For Jack, Millie, Joshua and Fabian

A Red Fox Book

Published by Random House Children's Books
20 Vauxhall Bridge Road, London SW1V 2SA

A division of The Random House Group Ltd
London Melbourne Sydney Auckland
Johannesburg and agencies throughout the world

The Random House Group Limited supports The Forest Stewardship
Council® (FSC®), the leading international forest-certification organisation.
Our books carrying the FSC label are printed on FSC®-certified paper.
FSC is the only forest-certification scheme supported by the leading
environmental organisations, including Greenpeace. Our
paper procurement policy can be found at
www.randomhouse.co.uk/environment

THE RANDOM HOUSE GROUP Limited Reg. No. 954009

www.randomhouse.co.uk

ISBN 0 09 941706 5

MIX
Paper from
responsible sources
FSC® C018072

Printed and bound in Great Britain by Clays Ltd, St Ives PLC

The MEGAMOGS in Moggymania

Peter Haswell

RED FOX

The Megamogs meet The Horrordogs

One afternoon, the Megamogs
came out of the Great White Shark
fish and chip shop licking their lips.

'Right,' said Kevin Catflap,
their captain. 'We've had a wicked
wodge of fish and chips. Now let's
get back to Miss Marbletop's and
see what she's got for our tea.'

Miss Marbletop was waiting on the doorstep of her quaint old cottage. 'Hello, Megamogs!' she cried. 'Guess what? I've got a big surprise for you.'

'Ooh!' exclaimed Tracy Tinopener. 'I like surprises.'

The Megamogs trooped in.

'I'd like you all to meet D.B.,' said Miss Marbletop. 'The poor chap was homeless. So he's come to live with us. I'm sure you'll all be very good friends.'

The Megamogs stared at D.B.

D.B. glared back.

'Everybody outside,' muttered
Kevin. 'We've got talking to do.'
Outside...

'Hmm,' said Glitzy Mitzy,
'I wonder what D.B.
stands for?'

'Oh, come on, Kev,'
said Tracy Tinopener. 'We've got
to give him a chance.'

And so the Megamogs gave
D.B. a chance, and this is what
happened next...

All week…

While D.B. lazed, lounged and had the time of his life…

the Megamogs looked gloomily on.

Then Miss Marbletop
announced that she was going on
one of her famous trips.

The Megamogs carried her bags
to the airport.

'For the next two weeks I'll be
on safari in Africa,'
she said.

'While I'm away,
I expect you to take good
care of D.B. Give him his bickies,
take him for walkies and get him
off to beddy-byes early.'

Miss Marbletop flew off. And when the Megamogs returned home, this is what was waiting for them...

'Shove off, you mangey Mogs,' growled D.B. 'The Horrordogs have moved in!'

Night after night...

The Horrordogs rock 'n' rolled, boogied and bopped, hollered, howled, yelled and yowled. The sounds of crashing and bashing, mad-dog music and furniture smashing went on until dawn.

Day after day…

The Horrordogs chilled out, flaked out, lounged, lazed and lay about by the pool.

'Come on, Kev,' said Glitzy Mitzy wearily. 'Let's do something to cheer ourselves up. Let's go down to the Great White Shark for a fish and chip binge.'

But when the Megamogs got there, they were in for a surprise. The Great White Shark fish and chip shop had closed down.

'That's the last straw,' griped Derek Dogbender. 'We've been bunked into the bushes, shoved up on the roof, and now we've got nowhere to go in town.'

'Right then, you Megamogs,' growled Kevin. 'We're going to do something. And guess what? It's going to be BIG!'

Next day...

Around the pool, the
Horrordogs were loafing and
lounging in their usual dumb,
doggy style, when out of the
bushes strode Kevin Catflap.

He climbed up to the diving
board. He paused, poised and

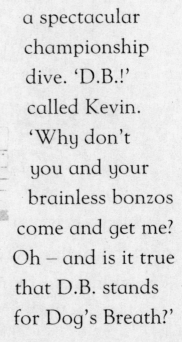 posed. Then he did
a spectacular
championship
dive. 'D.B.!'
called Kevin.
'Why don't
you and your
brainless bonzos
come and get me?
Oh – and is it true
that D.B. stands
for Dog's Breath?'

'I'll have you, Flatcap – I mean Catflap!' roared D.B. 'Come on, you dogs –

GET HiiiiM!

With howls of fury, D.B. and the Horrordogs hurled themselves into the pool.

Then out of the bushes came a great white shark. It plunged into the pool and…

powered by Moggypower, began to thunder after the Horrordogs.

The Horrordogs swam for their lives. They swam and swam...

they swam, swam, swam and swam...

then they
scrambled
out, scooted
and scrammed.

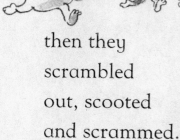 

One week later...

Miss Marbletop returned. 'Hello, Mogs!' she cried. 'I've brought someone to live with us. His name is Hugh G. Trunk. But I call him...

A Fight at the Opera

One morning the Megamogs were sitting outside Miss Marbletop's quaint old cottage when Derek Dogbender said, 'Where's Glitzy Mitzy today?'

At that moment Glitzy Mitzy appeared on the doorstep.

'*Darlings*,' she cooed, 'I've got some fan*tas*tic news. I've been talent spotted. Isn't that perfectly *marvellous?*'

'Yes,' she continued. 'Madame Una Cornetto has chosen me as her special pet.'

'Madame *who?*' asked the Megamogs, together.

'The great opera singer,' replied Glitzy. 'They call her "The Divine Diva". Of course, I've been expecting something like this to happen. It's nothing more than a girl of my breeding deserves.'

At that moment, a huge limo swept up. Madame Una stepped out and scooped up Glitzy.

'Darleeng pussy-wussy!' she cried. 'Say toodle-oo to your shabby tabby friends.'

'Toodle-oo!' cried Glitzy. 'From now on it's bright lights and heavenly nights all the way for me!'

The Megamogs were devastated.

'Our Glitzy's gone, Kev,' wailed
Tracy Tinopener. 'What are we
going to do now?'

'Dunno, Trace,' replied Kevin.
'We'll just have to wait and see.'

And so Glitzy began to lead a
life of glamour...

Back at Miss Marbletop's...

The Megamogs and Miss M. were switching channels when up popped a chat show. The guests were Madame Una and Glitzy.

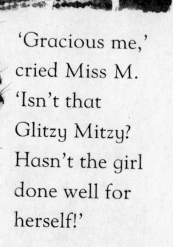

'Gracious me,' cried Miss M. 'Isn't that Glitzy Mitzy? Hasn't the girl done well for herself!'

One afternoon...

The Megamogs were mooching around a big store when suddenly they were swept aside by the manager.

And guess who came marching through?

'Yoo hoo, Glitzy!' cried the Mogs.

But Glitzy's eyes were so full of stardust she didn't even see them.

Then, one day...

Glitzy was wandering through Madame Una Cornetto's mansion.

Suddenly she saw something.

The next moment...

Madame Una arrived.

'My dear Marquis De Luxe,' she cried, 'how can I thank you enough for giving me such a cute poochi-woochi... I *lurve*-a heem! I shall call heem Pom-Pom!'

'Excellent!' exclaimed the Marquis. Then he sneezed.

'Pardon, Madame,' continued the Marquis. 'But I fee-ur zat I am allergeek to cats.'

Madame Cornetto glared at Glitzy Mitzy.

'Glitzy!' she commanded. 'Go to zer keetchen at once. Zer butler will geeve-a you some meelk.'

Glitzy was gutted! Completely shattered, she shuffled out of the room.

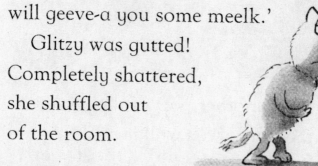

That night, at Madame Una's mansion...

The Megamogs were waiting and watching in the shadows.

In another part of the grounds, the Butler was walking two huge guard dogs.

'Look!' whispered
Derek Dogbender.
'There's Glitzy!'

The Megamogs
gazed up at their
friend.

Then, suddenly,
from the french
windows, the
sound of a piano
was heard.

A powerful
female voice began
to boom out.

29

The Megamogs crept closer and this is what they saw...

On a pouffe by the piano posed Pom-Pom the poodle.

Suddenly Pom-Pom spotted the Megamogs.
Pom-Pom stared at Kevin. Kevin glared at Pom-Pom.

Then Pom-Pom started yelping, yipping and yowling.

 *In the grounds…*
The Butler
stared into the
night. Then he let
loose his dogs.

The Megamogs made a dash for it.

Next day...

'Listen,' said Tracy. 'Here's what it says in *Yoohoo!* magazine:

"Divine Diva, Madame Una Cornetto, has a new pet called Pom-Pom. Madame Una says: My new opera opens on Saturday night and I have booked a special box for Pom-Pom so that he can watch me perform." '

Kevin Catflap
looked thoughtful.
Then he said:

'Right, I want you all to get out
your capes, coronets and other
clobber and get set to shimmy
out in
style.'

'What are we going to do, Kev?'
asked Derek Dogbender.

'We're going for a fight at the
opera,' said Kevin.

'Don't you mean a *night* at the
opera?' asked Tracy Tinopener.

'No,' said Kevin. 'I mean a
fight. So come on, you Mogs –
get done up to the nines and
togged out like toffs. We're going
to give that Pom-Pom a right old
fight – and guess what? It's going
to be BIG!'
*Saturday night, the grand opera
house...*

While Madame Una sang
with passion...

and the Megamogs enjoyed
the performance…

Kevin studied the audience. And
this is what he saw…

'Right,'
whispered
Kevin. 'There
he is…

so come
on, you
Mogs. *Let's
get him!*'

While the Megamogs crept out
of their box, Madame Una carried
on singing.

Then, suddenly,
another voice
was heard –
the voice of
Pom-Pom.

As Pom-Pom made a dash for
it... the Megamogs made a dash
for Pom-Pom. Out of the box...
through the orchestra pit... up the
ropes... to the top
of the scenery

and down the
scenery again.

Madame Una fainted.

The audience went wild.

A few seconds later, Pom-Pom dashed out through the stage door and hid in a dustbin.

The Megamogs followed him. But when they got outside, there was no sign of Pom-Pom.

'Call me an old pessimist, Kev,' said Derek, 'but we seem to have lost him.'

Suddenly the dustbin sneezed.

And as Derek Dogbender lifted the lid, Kevin grabbed Pom-Pom.

Next morning...

The Megamogs waited with Pom-Pom outside Madame Una Cornetto's mansion.

The Butler came out with Glitzy Mitzy. He handed her over and Kevin handed back Pom-Pom.

'About time,' said Glitzy. 'What kept you?'

Next day...

'Listen,' said Kevin, 'there's going to be a talent contest to find new TV stars. How about it, you Mogs? We could be famous, on TV, life of luxury. Tell you what, we could form a singing group – The Spicemogs – or maybe...'

'Oi,' shouted Kevin. 'Come back, everybody, we could all be superstars...

in fact, we could be…

The Knitathon

Duncan McDunk was worried. His customers were all going to Miss Marbletop's Dainty Doughnut shop.

'Those devilish Dainty Doughnuts are much too delicous,' he muttered. 'If I don't do something fast, they could put me out of business…

but what
can I do?'

I NEED A DIRTY, DASTARDLY IDEA - AND - AHA! I'VE GOT ONE!

That afternoon...

Miss Marbletop and Tracy
Tinopener were shopping. When

they got back
to the car park,
Miss M.'s red
sports car had
a flat tyre.

At that moment, McDunk
swept up in his limo and
offered the ladies a lift.

But when they
got into the car,
they were in
for a shock.

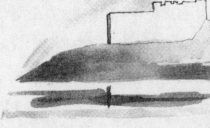

'D.B.,' snarled McDunk. 'Start driving!'

'Where to, boss?' asked D.B.

'My old castle on Loch Ness...

the dank
and dark Castle
Dunk!'

Back at the pool...

While the Mogs waited for Miss M. and Tracy, Kevin got on his mobile and ordered some pizzas.

Meanwhile...

McDunk and his prisoners arrived at Castle Dunk. The Horrordogs were waiting to greet them. They locked Miss Marbletop and Tracy in the tower. Then McDunk drove furiously back to his doughnut shop. *That night...*

D.B. brought the prisoners their supper.

D.B. got on his mobile and ordered a feast for himself and his canine cronies.

Then, while Miss M. chatted to D.B., Tracy pinched his mobile and called Kevin Catflap.

And so the Megamogs headed
up to Castle Dunk.
Next morning...
   'All right, you Horrordogs!'
called Kevin. 'We're sending in
a messenger to talk terms. Now...

I need a
volunteer to go in.
Barry Binliner –
come here!'

And so their messenger went
into the castle
with a message.

But the Horrordogs
weren't fooled...
and a few minutes
later, the messenger
came back
out again.

'Hmm,' said Kevin. 'That didn't work. Let's try something *musical*.'

So that afternoon the Megamogs disguised themselves as a pipe band and did a highland fling outside the castle door.

But the Horrordogs weren't
fooled. They hauled up the
drawbridge.

'All right
then,' said
Kevin. 'Let's try
something *spooky.*'

So that night the Megamogs
disguised themselves as ghosts.
Then they crept into the castle by
a back door and tried to scare
the Horrordogs.

But still the
Horrordogs weren't
fooled. Once again they threw
the Megamogs into the moat.

'Right,' said Kevin Catflap. 'I've had enough of castles, moats and porridge oats.

We're going home.'

So the Megamogs went back to Miss Marbletop's quaint old cottage. All the next day they sat around moping.

Suddenly,
Kevin Catflap
spoke up.
'Right, you
Mogs,' he said.
'This is what
we're going to do.
We're going to capture McDunk
then exchange him for Miss
Marbletop and Tracy.'

'How are we going to capture
McDunk, Kev?' asked Derek
Dogbender.

'We're going,' said Kevin,
'to throw a net over him.'

'A net?' gasped the
Megamogs.

'It'll have to be a big net,'
said Gary Gristle, doubtfully.

'No, Gary,' replied Kevin.

'It's not going to be big. It's going to be 'NORMOUS!'

The Megamogs looked dubious.

'Nice idea, Kev,' said Ginger Brownsauce. 'But where are we going to get a 'normous net?'

'That's simple, Ginger,' said Kevin. 'We're not going to *get* a 'normous net, we're going to *knit* a 'normous net!'

So the Megamogs went down to the wool shop and came back with bags bulging with balls of wool.

'Right,' said Kevin. 'No losing the thread or dropping stitches, woolly tangles or other hitches. Today we're going to make a 'normous net. So come on, you Mogs – pick up your needles and KNIT!'

KNIT ONE...
PEARL ONE...

And so the Megamogs knitted. They knitted and knitted. Then, in the dead of night, they crept along to McDunk's flat and yelled: 'FIRE! FIRE!'

'Help!' wailed McDunk. 'What am I to do?'

'Jump for it!' shouted the Megamogs. 'Don't be afraid – we've got a 'normous net!'

And so McDunk jumped.

'Now,' cried Kevin, 'you potty punk, you hunk of junk, you chunk of gunk, you load of bunk, you're sunk. Because now you're well and truly NETTED!'

The Megamogs slung the net
under their waiting helicopter.
Then they flew off to
Castle Dunk.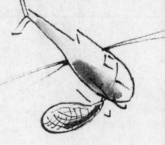

As the Megamogs
hovered with McDunk
dangling below, the
Horrordogs rushed to the ramparts.

'We want Miss M. and Tracy in exchange for McDunk,' said Kevin.

'I don't geddid,' growled D.B. 'Wot are those creepy cats doin' wif the Boss?'

'Don't ask daft questions,' yelled McDunk. 'Just do what he says and let the ladies go!'

And so...

Miss Marbletop and Tracy walked free. And at that moment...

the 'normous net broke.

Next day...

'That was nice
knitting,' said Kevin,
as the Megamogs
lounged by the pool
at Miss Marbletop's quaint
old cottage once again. 'In fact,
it's given me an idea...

you know what we're going to do?
We're going to get into the
Guinness Book of Records. And
guess how? We're going to do a
Knitathon. And not just any
Knitathon. This is going
to be the most

'NORMOUS KNITATHON the
world has ever seen. So come on,
you Mogs, get out your needles,
and start winding your wool.
Because it's time to get…

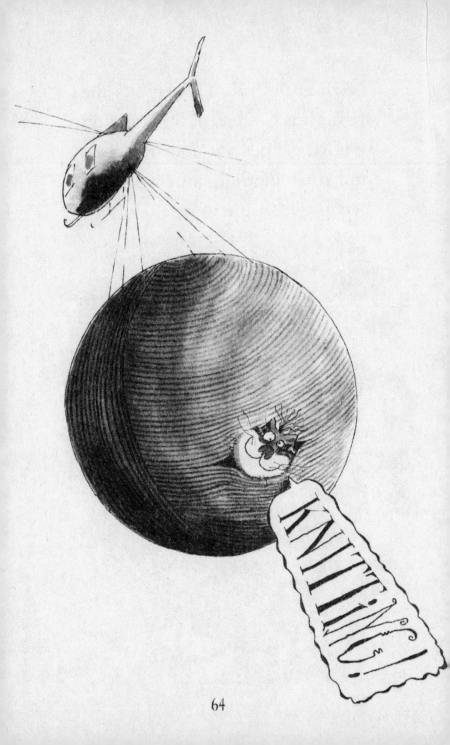